Blue Suburbia

Also by Laurie Lico Albanese

Lynelle by the Sea

Blue Suburbia

Almost a Memoir

LAURIE LICO ALBANESE

Perennial

An Imprint of HarperCollins*Publishers*

HarperCollins books may be purchased for educational, business, or sales promotional use. For information please write: Special Markets Department, HarperCollins Publishers Inc., 10 East 53rd Street, New York, NY 10022.

FIRST EDITION

Designed by Elias Haslanger

Library of Congress Cataloging-in-Publication Data

Lico Albanese, Laurie.
    Blue suburbia : almost a memoir / Laurie Lico Albanese.—
1st ed.
        p. cm.
    ISBN 0-06-056563-2
    1. Problem families—Poetry. 2. Parent and child—Poetry.
3. Abused children—Poetry. 4. Suburban life—Poetry. 5.
Women—Poetry. 6. Girls—Poetry. I. Title.

PS3562.I324B56 2004
811'.54—dc21

                                                    2003050942

04 05 06 07 08 ❖/RRD 10 9 8 7 6 5 4 3 2 1

Contents

Manhattan Awakening

Looking for Love

A New Life

Grief

Growing Pains

Still, Joy

Fate

Epilogue

Tell all the Truth but tell it slant.
—*Emily Dickinson*

Prologue

Blue Suburbia, Aerial View

Follow the highway
from Kennedy Airport
out to Grumman's old factory

see the used car lots,
strip malls, body shops,
rusted swing sets,
red rooftops, yellow
school buses

come closer,
peer in through our kitchen window
on Christmas Eve

watch Dad
putting together a tricycle,
Mom frying sausage
for turkey stuffing

listen to my sister snoring
baby whimpering
Dad cursing
neighbors shouting
with whiskey in their blood

see me putting out
a plate of snacks
for Santa

waking up
to find stacks of presents
under the tree

hear me asking
how the fat man
and his reindeer
fit through our window

see my mother
puffy-eyed
dragging on her cigarette

saying, *never you mind*
you are too damn smart
for your own good.

Tales from Childhood

The Story of My Life

First thing is the belt
worn soft from my father's pant loops
curling like a black eternity glyph
across my legs,
pliant back of my thighs,
hard shin of my calves

in bed, almost always in bed
almost always in the dark
the strap in his fist

or standing in the middle of my bedroom
drawing leather in a whisper
from the waist of his pants

at least three times a week
for five years or more
that's seven hundred times—
I know, he taught me math
the same way

because I was stubborn
he says, *the belt was a mercy,*
if I'd used my hands
I would have broken
your bones.

I love my father.

How can I tell the story of my life
without starting here?

219 Maple Street

We lived next door to a crazy family.
In the end
they left the house to the dogs,
locked the lady up,
and sold the land at auction.

A wrecking crew
removed the bathtub full of dog shit,
carried a rotting duck carcass
out of 219 Maple Street,
tore sinks from the walls
to erase the urine stink.

The place was a curse
and I'll tell you why.

It wasn't crazy Bobby
sweeping the carport roof by moonlight,
or the rusty garbage cans
his mother ran over
when she backed down her driveway
fifty miles an hour in reverse.

It wasn't the stinger
in Bobby's mouth
from a wasp on his Ritz cracker

it wasn't the puppy tied outside,
licking my fingers through chain link.

Go back,
even before somebody hit Bobby's dad
over the head
with a radio
in the heat of an argument
about loud music—

do you think I could make this up?

the man dropped stone dead
in sight of his own front stoop.

But go back, before he died.

See Caroline's family
renting Bobby's house
the year I turn seven

watch skinny Caroline
slinking through the yard
in hot pants
through heat waves
and thunder

see her father
naked under a towel
putting one foot up on the picnic bench
behind 219 Maple Street

asking me to follow him
into the house
alone

his long fingers
trying to part my thighs

his moan

his eyes
watching me
through the picture window
of 219 Maple Street.

Five Best Ways to Maim a Man

When the jailhouse comes to town,
my dad knows his time is here

he's been saving up for years,
waiting on a son—
having none
he drags me to the den
after Mom's gone to the mall,
tells me, *this is the way
it was in the war*

he says, *gooks, commies,
slant eyes
slit throats
wires thin and taut
across the sentry's night-blind eyes*

my dad is just getting started

he says I need to know
some things about men
especially now
that they are building the jailhouse
right across from my school,
any inmate with half a brain
and somebody to bribe

could run across the cauliflower fields,
duck under barbed wire,
hide near the bleachers
I pass every day.

I am nine years old.
I listen
with my mouth shut.

Dad says it only takes five pounds of pressure
to break the bone on top of the foot

he says if someone comes toward me
with intent to harm
I should jam my fingers into his nostrils
and pull,
use my thumbs
to gouge out his eyes,
hit up at his nose
with the heel of my hand,
driving the cartilage
right into his brain

go for the groin if there's no other choice

my dad tells me this because he loves me,
he tells me because my time is coming,
he tells me because a jailhouse is going up
and who knows what could happen next.

Sisters

I have two little sisters—

one is a baby
the other
shares my bedroom

Diana is the good girl
and I am bad

we have white wicker headboards
pink beaded lamps
hanging on chains
over nightstands

Diana talks in her sleep,
follow that ice cream truck,
save the last piece of bologna
for me.

We play
bite-your-finger in the dark,
I am good at catching her pointer
between my teeth,
slapping my hand over her mouth
to muffle the cries

she tries
keeping up with me in daylight
but I move fast

hide in the garage
when the red-haired Murphy girl
pounds a dark handprint
on my sister's back

pedal like fury
when the big boys
chase us home.

Second Thing

First thing is the belt

second thing is pouring Ajax
into Dad's dirty palms
when he washes after work

all-white-food diet
when his ulcer
acts up

my father opening
our electricity meter,
spinning the numbers
backward

doing the same thing
with the odometer
before selling the old
Ford

doubling
the size of our house
from the ground
up

paying the crane operator
only to dig the foundation

filling it
with his own hands
and forty pounds
of flesh

working nights
under spotlights
in his pajamas.

Independence Day

A gaggle of skinny cousins
drunk on pool water
and the pollens of summer
flop onto our dark carpet of lawn
to wait—

orange Creamsicles
drip down our arms,
mosquitoes come to feast

hairy dads
in baggy bathing trunks
flip hamburgers all day

while our mothers
in one-piece suits
do the doggy paddle

streets hum
with small explosions,
fireflies open the light show

and we lie down
on the cool lawn
waiting to be lifted
onto the rooftop

waiting to be passed
up the ladder
from uncle to uncle

borne up by the same muscles
that strapped us

rough men, relaxed now
by chlorine and Pabst Blue Ribbon
hoisting us
onto pebbly shingles

hoisting us
up to the high ledge
over the yard

our bare legs
scissoring the night air

our hearts pounding

our mothers prattling
somewhere far, far
below us

while we gaze up
into a sky
flaming with wonder.

Just Shake, and Bake

Am I adopted?
I ask my mother

she shrugs
hands me a bag of bread crumbs
drops in a pork chop

while in my other life
a girl who looks like me
is walking home from school

twirling her house key
turning the doorknob
opening the back door

finding her mother in the kitchen
smiling.

Sixth-Grade Infinity

Mr. Schultz teaches us infinity
by twisting a long strip of paper,
stapling the ends,
tracing the loop
inside-outside-inside-outside
without ever lifting
a finger from the surface

this is the year
I stare into the mirror
repeating *I am me, I am me, I am
me*

my mother hugs me
once
when my period begins

Mr. Schultz tells us
a man's ear freezes
on a cold day in Minneapolis—
when he goes through
a revolving door
the ear snaps off,
someone chases after him
calling, *I have your ear*

afterward
when the man hears
grass moaning
as he mows the lawn,
he lets the blades grow
waist-high

the grass sings
instead of screaming
the infinity of the universe
revolves

my face
floats like a moon
in the mirror.

Catcher in the Rye

I read anything
I can get my hands on

Old Yeller, Little Women
Black Beauty

Reader's Digest condensed novels
that turn up in our house
after Aunt Martha dies

Little House on the Prairie
Harriet the Spy
over and over again

my mother's hidden copy
of *The Happy Hooker*

and finally
Catcher in the Rye
all those phonies
those bastards
those assholes
lined up on the page
where I can count them,
savor them, run my fingers
over Holden's rage.

I Wish

I wish I didn't jackknife downstairs
for a clean pair of jeans

wish I didn't find my mother
lying on the old brown couch
weeping

cheeks wet and swollen,
hand across her eyes

I wish I didn't kneel beside her
to ask what was wrong

wish I didn't hear her say
you—

you're what's been
wrong with my life
for fourteen years.

What else is there
to wish for?

I stood up quickly
backed out of the room

grabbed my jeans
and ran.

Ignition

Ignition

I was fifteen
when I felt myself
ignite—

it wasn't one thing
like the back of a boy's neck
or my breasts waiting under wool
for sweaty palms to awaken their nipples

it wasn't the way I could buy a beer in Rudy's bar,
get behind the wheel of a car
and feel the gears shaking in my hands.

No. I ignited that spring
when I walked up and down the turnpike
looking for a job

hands folded behind my back,
fingers rubbing at the spark
each time someone said *sorry*
and I could hear my mother sneer.

I flew across the road heading west,
ribbon ripped from my hair
by the spray of oncoming trucks,
footprints dimming in dirt

until that boy on the Harley Davidson
put one dark boot in my path,
gunning his motor for me to alight

I slipped my legs around his hips,
dumping everything out of my handbag
right there

in front of the old Dairy Queen
I burst into flames
when I felt how fast
I could move away from home.

Motorcycle Matt

At last
my escape route

this handsome boy
with a beard
that makes my eyes
roll into the back of my head
when he rubs his chin
against my thighs

for fun
we take the Harley out to Jones Beach
turn off the headlights
ride fast
without helmets,
wind tearing our faces,
shrieks trailing behind us

this must be
him—

the man I'm going to marry

my first love
my first black eye

my second black eye

my third black eye.

Whiskey

My father asks—

I tell him I tripped.
I say I fell.
I say Matt hit me.

Dad turns pale
my mother
presses her lips together

in the morning
there is a liquor bottle
in the kitchen sink

I have never seen
my father drink whiskey
and I'm not sure
if this is my fault

until Mom spins around
and spits out
you are a fool
and a slut

I am planning my escape

I hiss back, *someday*
I'm going to be out there
in the world
and you'll still be stuck
in these same four walls.

Suddenly Lisa

Baby sister Lisa
says nobody remembers
her young life

and she's right

one day she was a squall
in my mother's arms,
the next day
she was nine

I barely paid attention to her—

I was too busy
searching for boyfriends
each of them promising
to care for me
more than Mom did

each one wiping tears from my face
each one whipping my longing into loss

and suddenly Lisa
throwing her whole body on top of mine
one night while I was crying

it may not sound like much
but to me it was a miracle

someone in my own family
holding me
holding me
because I hurt.

Accident, Part I

I snuck out of school
stuffed hash
into small ceramic pipes

slipped cartons of Marlboros
into my backpack
at the Shell station
while Helen stood guard

and that's only my early teens,
that's not false I.D.
quaaludes and rum
new disco on the turnpike
wet roads at four in the morning
foot on my father's accelerator

that's not jumping the divider
crossing four lanes of oncoming cars
shooting between two telephone poles
through a set of hedges
across the front lawn
into the living room wall
of a deserted brick house

that's what rebellion got me.

Accident, Part II

I passed out at the wheel
smashed into a house
totaled the car
was rushed to the emergency room

my father came at daybreak
to take me home

the next afternoon
when we saw the mess
I'd made of his Mercury—

hood folded like a pocketknife
windshield crackled like foil

—my father cried out

his chest rose and fell
he told the body shop
to scrap the car

mincemeat, he mumbled

he said nothing else
for the rest of the day

but we both knew
I could have died

I should have died

and instead
I'd been shown
a mercy.

Suicide

Diana tried to kill herself
the summer after my accident—

what were my parents
to make of all this?

Dad working overtime
to take us on vacation

Mom keeping the house clean,
kitchen stocked,
food cooked

everything orderly
except the girls
wanting to die
in different ways.

Diana took a bottle of gout pills
from Uncle Tommy's medicine chest,
washed them down with vodka

woke my father
in the middle of the night

said, *L—— gave me vodka*
I used it to swallow
some pills.

The doctors pumped her stomach
and recommended a counselor
who said Diana was crying out
for help.

What kind of help? my parents
asked each other. I heard them
over the hum of the attic fan.

This is crazy, they said,
we haven't done anything
wrong.

Acceptance

Dad's blue philosophy
can be summed up
in a few phrases—

FDR
ruined
this country.

Don't be
in such a hurry
to grow up.

I'm not to blame
for slavery.

Always finish
what you start.

My mother
thinks I'm too smart
for my own good

everybody in our family
is suspicious of
draft dodgers
psychologists

professors
doctors
lawyers
Liberals
and just about anybody
     with an education

so who encourages
me to apply to college?

I do it on my own.

Write to the state school
ask for a loan

and when the reply arrives
it says, *welcome
we'll see you in the fall.*

Five Words

Most days
I found my mother
standing at the kitchen sink

I'd come home from school
or walk in from the yard
where the Murphy boys
killed bumblebees
with their bare feet

my mother would turn
or not

mostly not

but I kept coming into the room
year after year

struggling to puzzle out
what I'd done
to stretch her spine
into that hard line.

Do you get the picture now?

Can you see her
at the sink

me waiting behind her
my heart—what?

not broken
it was too many years
to live with a broken heart

my heart
silent.

All this
leading to the day
I left for college.

Until then
my mother
had little to say.

I was seventeen.
Too smart for my own good,
I knew that much

thanks to Mr. Schultz
with his talk of singing grass
and his push toward infinity
I was launched

the car was packed
with cardboard boxes
two new pairs of jeans
notebooks, pens,
tea bags, peanut butter,
hot plate and pot
Dad bought
as a splurge
in the Army Navy
surplus store.

My father gripped the wheel.
Mom sat in the front seat
next to him.

I looked out the window
to watch our house
slide away

my mother's shoulders shook

I couldn't see
her whole face
you understand

just the short chop
of dark hair,
blue collar of her car coat
the slimmest line of cheek

but I was sure
my mother
was crying
because I was leaving home.

Dad slid the engine
into gear

I leaned forward
toward my mother

she must have heard
my breath in her ear
must have felt me
drawing near

she didn't turn
but said, in a voice
only I could hear

I'm so ashamed of you.

I didn't ask why—

years later
it's easy to say
you would have demanded
an explanation

but I was seventeen

blood rushed to my head
dread flew out of me in a sigh

the sky was autumn blue
my father's foot fell hard
on the gas pedal

the lash of unlove
unleashed me

with those five words
my mother released me
into the world.

S.U.N.Y. College

I work in the cafeteria
so I can buy books

call home
and hear my mother
silently hang up
the phone

drink beer
until I vomit
then go back
for more

read a letter
that says, *Mom*
won't let me
write to you
sorry, love
Dad

feel the hollow
of loneliness
at dusk

sit by the window
after midnight
highlighting notes

putting dreams
on a tiny scrap of paper
in a small corner
of my diary

I want to be
somebody.

Life Lessons

Campus is loaded
with skinny girls from Queens

girls with closets full of jeans
and parents who visit monthly
carrying casseroles and cash.

I don't know what I envy more,
the money
or the way those girls are cherished

while I stay up late reading Freud
sleep through *Beowulf*
put on a hairnet
and listen to my dorm mates
complain about the food.

My boss at the dining hall
is a Buddhist
grad school dropout
who tells me
we should all strive
for the beauty
of nothingness

but I already feel like nothing
walking across campus
invisible

barely breathing but getting by
getting B's

going home
to a summer job
at Alexander's department store

carrying a notebook
full of stories, full of poems

my mother says
I am full of myself
but her words wash over me
like air.

Manhattan Awakening

←

Job Interview

In a fifty-dollar brown suit
bought with my employee discount
I pack my résumé
ride the railroad
tuck the *New York Times* under my arm
take the subway uptown
walk from Madison to Broadway
searching for Sixth Avenue.

Back and forth
biting off lipstick
barely holding down breakfast
I look for the street
that should logically fall
between Seventh Avenue and Fifth.

Do they count differently
in the city? Could Sixth Avenue
somehow be on the other side of
Second?

Double-checking the address
and interview time,
weeping in front of Radio City,
I rush up to a policeman

who pushes back his hat
points to the sign overhead,
says, *Avenue of the Americas
is Sixth Avenue*.

Heaving in the elevator
brushing my hair
smoothing on blush
I wonder how I'll ever get
where I want to go.

The Test

I type
one hundred words
per minute

so fast
I fill the paper
and still there is time left
on the clock.

This is how I become
an editorial assistant

but I have other plans

fast fingers
working hands
bigger plans.

Prelude: In My Studio

Mornings
on the subway platform
watching faces flash past
I imagine myself rounding the tracks,
a beacon ahead of the light.

Even before my parents met
I was on my way here.

Even before my father
drove the ice cream truck
down the block
where my mother baby-sat
in pedal pushers,
brushing dark hair
off her forehead,
yelling at the little ones
to stay off the road.

She was only thirteen—
the egg of me was buried inside her,
my soul had not yet spoken.

Anything might have happened
in the next five years—
the boy driving the truck

could have died in the Korean War,
the dark-haired girl
might have been beaten once too often
with a high-heeled shoe,
learned to stand up for herself,
gone to college
instead of to the firehouse dance
where their romance began

lost the clip that glittered in her hair
and drew my father to her.

While the city's white lights
cascade across my notebook
I lay in bed at night
writing the history
that brought me to this day.

Real Men Don't Eat Quiche

The editor who publishes
the bestselling book
about quiche and machismo
has a corner office, four phone lines,
a wife, two kids, and a dozen
assistants who burst into tears
several times a week.

He flosses while discussing budgets,
has his shoes shined during meetings

he doesn't know my name
but I knock on his door,
ask if there's some more *literary task*
I might take on—
not that buying gin for I. B. Singer's party doesn't satisfy me,
not that clearing the way for V. C. Andrews's wheelchair
isn't a thrill.

He adjusts his eyeglasses,
says he likes my moxie,
selects a box
from the bottom stack.

Clutching opportunity against my chest
I go home, change into sweatpants,

unplug the telephone, make a tuna sandwich,
sit down to discover
he has given me
pornography—
a soft manuscript
shameful enough
to put me in my place

my face burns
but I read every word
write up the report
put it on his desk
first thing Monday morning:

this manuscript
containing vivid scenes of bondage
and sadism
is misogynist in tone
which may be offensive
to the largely female consumers
of nonillustrated soft porn

thereafter
the editor greets me
by name.

In the Museum of Modern Art
(*on seeing Picasso's* Guernica)

The first time I stood in front of a Picasso
his anger struck me like horses' hooves,
the cacophony of battle choking me with terror,
gray and red figures silencing me with addled apprehension
until I could only shift in my new loafers,
straining to hear the allusions of fine-boned people
whispering in the museum's hush,
fissures of history hissing off their tongues
while I struggled to name
loud music thrumming my heart,
passionate beating of a silent mantra
galloping through my chest

(*I'll never catch up, I'll never catch up*)

I'll never catch up
because I am a daughter of blue suburbia
raised on Campbell's soup casseroles
and cans of crispy onions,
I have run my hand over cross-stitched pillowcases,
ridden a motorcycle through Maryland,
climbed out my bedroom window
but never been to Spain,
never spoke in the tongues of Cubist despair
nor misted at a grandmother straining to see the *Pietà*

and nothing prepared me
for the day I stood face-to-face with genius,
hearing the man's message
screaming in my soul
but afraid to say a word.

Looking for Love

Nine Ways to Midnight

Simon
the uncircumcised

Sam
who wants to
spank me

Micky
who tickles me
in bed

Micky's friend Bill
whose nose bled
on my blanket

Paul
whose last girlfriend
was a junkie

Dave
who is still in love with
Holly
who is in love with
Jill

Stephen
who wants to know
if prep school
was an option

Kris
who never pays

Bryan
who says he might
love me soon.

Married Man

I almost can't stand it—
I want to know you so badly,
not only how you look
in the room with me
but how you look at your wife
while she is cooking dinner,
where you sit when you read the newspaper
what you do after midnight
when I am slipping into bed
or already sleeping,
dreaming of standing with you
under an umbrella,
holding you after your hair has turned white
I almost can't stand it
wondering how far your fingers
would stretch across the dark
to turn off the light
I almost can't stand it—

Pregnant

First it's the blue dot
on a plastic stick
that my pee turns pink

then it's a small brick
building, the sink
of formaldehyde

dizzy
on an empty stomach
in an airless room

one last chance
to change my mind

(I think,
Bryan doesn't love me
but he might love me soon)

the walls are on wheels
bodies are weeping
in cots around me

hands rustle sheets,
fingers touch mine
skin on skin

in the dark
the way this all started

two by two
as if into the ark
we are pushed
under bright light

the howl of me
is unearthed

metal stink
of blood unbirthed
with the blade-
ache in my belly.

Hands

I was wearing pink cotton
and fake pearls,
dressed not as myself
but as someone softer

Nick crossed the room
shook my hand
at the hors d'oeuvres table

I have no idea
what I was saying
but my mouth was moving
he was smiling
so it must have been
all right

I must have seemed just fine
to this new man
with hard muscles
under his sports coat
and beautiful
     broad-boned
     clean, uncalloused
     hands

not nervous hands
not working hands

I folded up my fingers
hid my mangled cuticles
torn nails, gnawed skin

he didn't seem to notice
or maybe he didn't mind

reaching across the chasm,
pulling me toward him.

Nick

Over dinner
Nick tells me
about working in Alaska
one summer,
where he painted landscapes
on weekends
instead of going to bars.

Together
we paint a still life—
orange daylilies,
purple hyacinth, yellow
forsythia welcoming
spring.

In December
he comes to Long Island
where we decorate
my family's Christmas tree

Mom
puts lasagna in the oven,
pulls out the video camera
zooms in on Nick's hands

Nick's hands
hanging ornaments

that Dad rearranges
when Nick turns his back

because we always
hang the bright balls
in size order
from tiniest on top
to biggest on bottom

and I wonder
what would happen
if Dad just left them
randomly strung—

would the tree
tumble over?
would my parents
lose sleep at night?
would it be all right
if things were just
pleasant

but not
in their proper place?

I Hid

Nobody found me for years
they were too busy bowling,
bickering, hanging wallpaper

watching *Jeopardy!*
drinking pink wine
waiting for Christmas
and a new set of Corelle.

I hid in my closet
with the shoes,
in a snow fort
dug into the blizzard of '69

in the shadow of the jailhouse
for a whole summer
with Holden, Phoebe
and a bottle of calamine

I hid, no one saw me
until you came along
and we huddled under blankets
reading the unbearable lightness

your body bare on top of mine,
another place to hide

except you exhaled
and I sucked in your unused oxygen

your heart beat one deep gong
for every two notes of my own,
you pulled me naked
in front of the mirror

took my chin in your hands
said, *look*,
look

and I saw something
altogether new—
I saw my center
filling.

Leaving

The man
who gazed into my eyes
and said, *the closer you get
the better you look*

is being promoted
and moving to the
Midwest

now this
is the kind of love
I know—

wounded love

nothing left
to lose
love.

To say
I'll miss you
doesn't seem enough

so instead I ask
*does this
have to be
the end?*

Embers

In the middle of the night
Nick calls to tell me
about the hot July day
twenty years ago
when his father
came home from work
to eat lunch
with his family.

Closing my eyes
I hear Nick's voice
quiver

but what I see
are sprinklers pumping
charcoal in the barbecue
macaroni salad chilling

three boys, one small girl,
mother and baby
around the picnic table

Nick's father annoyed
because the boys are wild,
wanting only to cool themselves
in chlorine water

Nick's father pausing
when his wife suggests
he spend the afternoon swimming
instead of working

Nick's father driving back to the factory
where he is a chemical engineer

pulling into the parking lot
setting the hand brake
jingling coins in his pocket

entering the building
just before the explosion

his knees buckling

panic
then clear-eyed resolution
as he runs deeper
into the fire
to carry out a big fellow
who fainted.

I listen to Nick
but I wonder if his dad
thought of his little girl's
blue eyes
then.

I wonder
if his wife's face
flashed through
his mind.

I wonder
if he had something
he wanted to say to his sons
before he died.

I wonder
what will happen
if I dare to show Nick
my childhood wounds—

these scars
seen and unseen
are the embers of our lives.

A New Life

Solitaire Diamond

I am trying to imagine
what it will be like
to be married

to love and be loved
by this man
who reads thick history books
and runs a mile
under six minutes

this man
who rarely complains
who seems, some days
to conspire with angels

all of this
is novelty enough—

now Nick is offering me
a real release,
my true escape route
and a one-way ticket
to his apartment
near the zoo
in Chicago
where we make love

and listen to the lions
roar in their cages.

My escape, yes,
but what shape
do long days of love
take on?

For this
I cannot rely
on my father and mother
nor the cool chill, dry tears,
and slow burdened years
of their marriage.

Near the shore of Lake Michigan
where we paddle a purple kayak
off the Hyde Park jetty
I wake—
how can I say this?

I wake
some mornings
next to Nick
and fear this is the day
everything will shatter.

Housekeeping

So much happens at once—
I move to Chicago
we get married
get pregnant
buy a yellow brick bungalow
in the city,
near a river
that runs backward
from the lake
to the center of the land

put up wallpaper
in the nursery
where I yell at Nick,
waving the leveling tool
in my hand

until he asks, *why
are you yelling at me?*

and I can't think of a thing to say
except that I am yelling
because my parents always yelled
when they put up wallpaper.

The Next Generation

The moment of conception
changes not only my whole body
not only the rising of the sperm
to meet the egg
in an embrace that will grow
into the next generation—

the act of conception
joins me to my mother
in a way I could not have imagined.

While I lay with my belly
exposed to the sun
and watch it swell

read about the zygote expanding,
fingernails forming, eyelids fluttering

while I strip to the skin
in the heat wave of my eighth month
and clean the house
stark naked

make up my mind
to be kind
no matter what

this child might ever say
to me—

eight hundred miles away
my mother is collecting tiny T-shirts
sewing curtains for the nursery
buying miniature baby shampoos,
soft-bristled hairbrushes,
pearl-handled nail clippers,
maternity blouses

at a great distance from me
my mother is preparing herself
for joy.

Planting Bulbs

Trowel and shovel
gloves and towel

I bend and dig
plant and cover
water and rest

the day before
the day before
the baby is due

rooting myself to the earth
after three days of
slow labor

walking and waiting
breathing and sleeping
eating and bathing

sorting tulip,
daffodil, and hyacinth
bulbs

relishing easy toil
then scattering them
across the soil—

blanket of wood chips
warming the flower bed

Nick's fingers
lacing a lattice
under my belly

crayoned rainbow
underground
already moving
toward the light.

Due Date

Blood.

Hurry, hurry
to the hospital
leave the car at the curb
carry me up to the sliding doors

hold my hand, Nick
don't let anything happen
to the baby

don't leave me
don't let go of me

keep whispering
my name
while they put the needle
into my spine

I can't feel anything
Nick

I'm afraid.

We

welcome to the world
Melinda Rose

7 pounds, 11 ounces

excellent Apgar scores

Dancing Baby

I felt you dance into me.
Oh, some babies are borne
of hot, wide passion

others in momentary indifference
with untroubled sleep
the real reward.

But you danced in
with the moon waxed
and your daddy singing
a love song to the sky

a song with my name and yours
ribboning through it
until there was a chain so long
in a voice so strong

you had no choice
but to follow it
to join our joy
to dance into my belly

and rest untroubled
for nine lovely months
until you were ready to sing
your own love song.

Grandma

My mother
flies in from New York
the day we bring home
the baby

keeps busy
bathing Melinda
making meat loaf
scouring the kitchen
smiling

granddaughter
in her arms
my mother is
happy

how am I
to take this?

where did
this woman
come from?

where was she
when I was
young?

Summer

This is the day I live for—

morning sun on the tomato plants
wet grass dampening our feet
Melinda in the carriage

your back bare
as you bend over a screen
hammer it into shape
lift the ladder
step on the bottom rung

and rise.

Minding My Own Business

Nick is accepted
into business school

he'll have to
quit his job

we'll have to live off
our meager savings
for two years

Nick sees
opportunity

I see
the difference
between growing up
middle class
with the promise
of more to come

and growing up
in the shadow
of the jailhouse.

Man Enough

There, next to the car
is the scar
of our fight

a deep hole
from the night
Nick shouted at me

to back off, shut up
leave him alone
but I wouldn't

I followed him outside
until he slammed a fist
through the wall

Is this what you want?
Does this make you happy?
Is this man enough for you?

What is man enough for me
if not Nick
with his schoolbooks
and his glasses
and his cards
full of sloppy handwriting?

Nick
at the threshold
of our bedroom
with Melinda in his arms
and a dishrag
over his shoulder.

Nick in the hollow
of our garage
where we stand
under wood beams
near the dark hole

splintered, trembling

our past harms
done
and undone
again and again.

Grief

Good-bye

My father
didn't go to his father's deathbed
in Florida

Dad said,
if I fly down there,
he'll think he's
dying

my grandfather
was ninety-two

he knew
he was
dying

he knew
his son
didn't come
to say good-bye

only the two of them
knew why

maybe it had
something to do

with the way the old man
hit my dad
with a closed fist
year after year

or the fact
that he beat my grandmother
unconscious
and left her
on the kitchen floor

maybe that was all there was.

Housewife

It seems
I am a housewife
now

minutes at home creep past
but months fly by

Melinda is in pre-K,
I am trying to write freelance,
Nick is traveling often
for his new job

and when he comes home
we argue
because that is easier
than saying I am carrying
an ache of dread
in my chest

it rattles through me
like a chip off the stone
of my mother's misery

I don't expect pity

I am only
a lonely woman
spending too much time
at her kitchen sink—

the Chinese
are mowing down their own
in Tiananmen Square

I just read a poem
about the Salvadoran colonel
who dumped a bag
full of human ears
onto a dinner plate

I know there are worse fates
than mine
and yet I am wallowing
in the fear of years
like this

trembling under the kiss
of my mother's inheritance.

Multiplying

I am pregnant again
seeing a therapist
writing freelance

my mother called yesterday
and said, *I don't know
how to talk to the people
I love—*

then she told me
about the lump
in her chest

not sorrow
but the fleshy skein
of overgrowth

an abundance of cells
multiplying without instruction

a tumor in her lung
under the breast
wrapped around the rib

baby roiling in my belly
cancer coiling through my mother

voice of dread thickening
sickening me across the miles.

Lives Collide

I fly to my mother's side
with five-day-old Jack in my arms
and stitches between my legs

my mother lies
wrapped in a nylon robe

I say, *sometimes*
it's helpful
to have happy thoughts

cloudy-eyed
sipping soup
she says,
no one ever taught me

she gags a bit
I use a tissue
to wipe her spit

she says,
no one ever taught me
how to have a happy thought

my mother is fifty-three
her hair is still chestnut
her fingernails are painted red

she gags in bed
I nurse my newborn baby
fraught—

medicine bottles are cluttered
on the counter,
oxygen tanks stand clustered
near the fridge

my father is huddled
in the garage
tears pouring
down his cheeks

my mother is saying,
L——, *you are so lucky*

and even in the midst
of this sorrow, witness
to my parents' heartbreak

I can't help but whisper
into the nape of my baby's neck,

it wasn't luck
you know, Jack
I was determined to learn
how to be happy
before I died.

"Good Night, Mom"

I held your hand for hours
in a twilighted room
remarkable for its lack of odor,
smelling neither like medicine
nor like death
that came
with its back to the window

I sat near the bed
ignoring silent lips
on the TV overhead

I held your hand
our fingers became shadows,
dark spaces on a negative image,
the lost hollow behind bookshelves
where dust collects
and old photographs fall

I held on
ignoring the nurses' white jackets
and soft-soled shoes

I held on
until your limbs began to twitch,
legs flailing off the bed

I let go
because the doctor said
you might hold on
knowing I was there
you might hold on
even though there was no hope

I let go
when you couldn't blink
or swallow anymore

I left you
with newly polished fingernails
and a note written in huge letters
hung over your bed
in case you opened your eyes
one last time

they sent the note home in a bag
with six pairs of beige underwear,
books about beating cancer,
smooth white rosary beads,
and your new nightgowns
slit up the back.

How You Mourn a Mother

You lie in bed until the weight of the covers is a burden,
until the soles of your feet sting when they hit the floor.

You look in the mirror and think, *I look just like my mother.*
Then you open your closet and see the sweater she bought you,
the one you never liked. You put it on.

You cry in the car on the way to the grocery store
letting tears make dark circles on the thighs of your jeans.

You never mention this to friends.

When the phone rings you remind yourself,
that won't be Mom,
and on her birthday you stand in the cemetery
wishing you could ask her something simple
like whether she likes your new haircut,
and if it is worth praying at all in this life.

On Sunday you go to church to hear them talk about heaven,
and just after midnight you say,
this would be a good time, Mom.
Then you hold your breath and wait.

When She Comes to Me

In dreams my mother comes to me
   as she never did in life

humming along with the radio
   she puts one arm around my shoulders,

this is what my parents told me, she says,
   that I was nothing special, never would be

she doesn't cry when she tells me this
   but her voice goes high as a child's

her voice keeps going up and up.

Mirror

My mother didn't really say
I'd been ruining her life for fourteen years—
not there in the basement, anyway

it just fit so neatly
to say I found her crying
and she blamed me
with a sharp slap
on that sunny afternoon

what really happened is this:

I jackknifed downstairs
for a clean pair of jeans,
heard something in a dark corner
of the playroom,
froze when I saw my mother's
silhouette

Mom?

I crept closer
my mother came into focus—
white shorts, bare feet

lying on the couch
hand over her eyes
palm up
weeping

Mom? Are you all right?

Her left hand was damming the tears,
the other dangling off the old couch,
skimming the tiled floor. My mother's hands
were small, like mine, with soft nails
that split. She bit them, the way I do,
to trim the edges and cuticles.

I hadn't reached for my mother's hand in years.
Her fingers were pale and cool.

I'm so unhappy

her words flew to me—
my mother, unhappy enough
to be lying in the dark
weeping in the middle of
the afternoon

I'm so lonely

her words waver to me through time
breaking like waves over rocks.

Did you tell Daddy?

Surely, I thought, my father would
do something if he knew. My father

was a fixer, mender of broken things.
He would take her apart and make her whole again.

I can't tell him. He just gets mad.

She pulled her hand away then, or maybe
I let go. Maybe there was a noise in the kitchen
maybe one of my sisters called, maybe the
phone rang, I don't remember what ended it

don't know
if it ever ended.

Sometimes I still see my mother
lying in the basement
muffling her own sobs

sometimes
when I look in the mirror
I see her
looking back at me
through tear-rimmed eyes.

You see now
why it was easier
to say she lashed out at me
that day

you see now
why I forgive her.

Green Sleeves

Your coat hangs in my closet now
empty green sleeves filled with air,
two pennies and an old tissue
stuffed in one pocket, collar curved up,
perfume still scenting the plaid cuffs.

Does anyone remember I blew you a kiss
through the ambulance window?
The sky was bright above autumn leaves,
you tipped your face to the sun for the last time,
rode away without sirens into silence.

I don't think of you underground
but somewhere in the light,
gust of wind moving down the hallway,
a song on the other side

I strain to hear you.

Losing My Way

My Road Not Taken

I tell them *no*.
I have babies at home,
can't make this freelance job
full-time
can't climb that ladder
can't work five days
sometimes nights
weekends
mornings at my desk
with coffee and memos
office pals and press conferences
deadlines, headlines,
datelines—

stuff I've always wanted

and still want
so badly
that I drive home weeping
for the road not taken

weep
as I cook dinner
put in another load of laundry
read Melinda a story
change Jack's diaper

remind myself
this is a precious time
and all time
runs through our hands
like sand.

Back East

For years
I long to go back East
where the pace is familiar
and bagels taste best

but when the time arrives
there is not much heart
in my search for a house

I feign enthusiasm
when the moving van
delivers our furniture

a motley assortment
of strange pieces
out of place in Jersey

like worn feathers
on a newborn bird.

Fifteen-Year Cicadas

It starts with the cicadas
burrowing up from a fifteen-year hibernation

thousands of jackbooted bugs
crawling from the sarcophagus of soil
to mate in my backyard

like something out of Hitchcock
the air abuzz with raw shock of
constant sound.

Everyone says they are harmless.

I am already unhappy
to be back in the suburbs—
summer heat thrumming at first light

carcasses of spent insects
crunching underfoot
by the children's swing set

cadence of the drove's dance
drawing me deeper
into a death knell

mark the onset
of a throbbing anxiety
thickened by the restless earth—

and when the cicadas are gone
translucent wing shards swept up by wind
spiracle pieces slung into trees

I discover something in me
has become undone

so that even after the soil is patched
I hear
the steady munching of small mouths
gnawing their way back from underground.

Fight or Flee

The fear comes over me
while I am drinking tea
in my neighbor's kitchen
looking at Dith Pran's photo
of an iris garden
on the front page
of the newspaper

yes Dith Pran
of the killing fields
has been reincarnated
as a photojournalist

but that should not cause
tremors of fear
to shoot through me

there are only clean tiles
green teacups
early berries in a bowl

yet suddenly
I am terribly
afraid

my hands are numb
I hear blood

rushing to my head
cluttering my thoughts
cutting off sounds

my heart pounds
I look around

there is Dith Pran's photograph
on the kitchen counter
teakettle steaming
every cell in my body
screaming

fight or flee
fight or flee

and my neighbor
calmly drinking tea.

Six Months Later—

supermarket lights
quiver overhead

I rush in and out
without shopping.

Baby Jack
climbs out of his crib
while I am hiding
in the bedroom.

Melinda wails, *Mommy*
you made pasta
every night this week.

I cook chicken.

For six months
I'm afraid
when I answer
my front door

afraid to look up
in the grocery store

afraid to sit
at a parent-teacher
conference

afraid
when I meet
my own eye
in the mirror.

Panic

The fear takes over

even though I give away
all my crazy lady books

—if someone in the story
lands in the psych ward
wham, that book goes on
a pile in the corner—

I meditate, breathe
count backward
breathe

buy self-help books
instead of novels

chart my panic
by its intensity

take up yoga
wake at five
jog to the hilltop
pray to the oak

carry quartz crystals
in my bra

see a therapist
who keeps a parrot
in her office

go to church
beg for God's intervention

drink vodka
on the rocks

call Nick
at the office
call Nick
at the office

recite a mantra in my head
(*every day, in every way,*
I am getting better and better)

still
the fear
keeps coming.

Endurance

I am
barely
hanging
on

getting sicker
and sicker

thinner and thinner

drenched in sweaty
insomnia

wrenched with fear
of just about
everything

especially
fear of being
alone

and fear
of being
with anyone
else

fear
of the very life
being sucked
out of me

the way
it was sucked
out of my mother

the very life
of a wife
in the suburbs

with a house to keep up
and a husband
who's gone all day

the very life
I fought to be free of—

barely
hanging
on

fearing
the fear

day and night
for more than
a year.

On the Couch

When at last
I see the doctor
I am prone
across his couch
sobbing

Jack is running in circles
around the waiting room
my hair is in tangles

*Do you swear
you can help me?*

The doctor hesitates.

*If you can't help me,
then put me in the hospital*

He looks at me.

He doesn't write
anything down.

I tell him,
I am a resilient person.

I tell him,
I love my family.

I tell him
about the belt
the neighbor
the accident
the cancer
the road not taken
the panic.

He gives me
three prescriptions:

one to take immediately
one to take at bedtime
one to take upon rising
before I call him
in the morning.

The Doctor Helps Me See

It wasn't up to me
to teach my mother
how to be happy.

I was never
too smart
for my own good.

It's all right
to feel insecure—

it's not a contradiction
to feel insecure
and to be strong.

Living with uncertainty
is not only possible
but necessary.

Medicine
is neither
the right answer
nor the wrong
one.

To be a woman
with children
does not condemn me
to my mother's fate.

I have already traveled
far from home.

But look at where I am,
I tell him,
I am sitting in your office
whining.

No, no.
He shakes his head.
You are finding
your own way.

Out of the Blue

←

What Saved Me?

Anxiety is a paradox,
a box without a door.

Fearing that fear
will never go away
is both a symptom of the illness,
and the illness itself.

Time
and a lucky dose of medicine
dissolve the box
bit by bit

the walls thin
a little light comes in
you start sleeping longer at night

you carry tranquilizers in your purse and
one day realize you haven't looked for them
in a week

you dread every morning
and one day
when the dread is a lump in your throat
instead of a horse race in your heart
you remember to be thankful.

Work saved me.
My doctor saved me.
Nick saved me.
Medicine saved me.

Thinking about life in a long
continuum saved me.

Praying saved me.

Kelly, Laura, and Amy,
who took my phone calls day or night
saved me.

My mother-in-law,
who slept on my couch
when I thought I was
dying, saved me.

What saves anybody?

Faith saved me.

Romans 8 saved me: *Now hope*
that is seen is not hope. For who hopes
for what is seen? But if we hope
for what we do not see, we wait for it
with patience.

Faith, hope, and love saved me.

Hangdog determination
and the arc of time
that cures almost every illness
saved me.

One morning
after two years of anxious agony
I was standing in my bathroom
putting on mascara
and I wasn't a woman with a mantra, I wasn't
a woman swallowing air
I did not have lungs that wouldn't fill
I had no nonstop string of questions
ringing my brain
I wasn't staring at myself in the mirror
looking for the crack in my composure
that would reveal my illness to the world

I was just a 38-year-old woman
putting on her makeup,
wiping a stray fleck of mascara
off her eyelid, slipping on her shoes,
locking the front door,
stepping outside into an
ordinary
glorious day.

Working Again

I nearly panic
during the interview,
bite a piece of pill
for good luck,
now I'm a reporter
at the local newspaper

hardly minding
the mayor and his cronies
offering me old crackers
when I cover their
country club party

understanding
the local garbagemen
don't know that my stories
help save their jobs

shrugging off
angry glares
of people who object
to our coverage of the electric trains
and what they'll bring
when the tracks plow through town

reporting
is the manic fulfillment

of all that I have
struggled through

empowerment
comes from being a big fish
in a small pond

and I don't mean
the kind that has to float at the bottom
during winter
to stay alive.

The Fine Edge

Few people seem to know
that as a young man
Abraham Lincoln
had a little nervous breakdown

Einstein labored round the clock
perfecting his theory of relativity,
spent the next year in bed
and was never the same

Winston Churchill napped
to help him manage mania

Dickinson and Munch
were afraid to
cross their thresholds

St. Francis
took off all of his clothes
and walked through Italy

Sir John Gielgud
suffered such social anxiety
that he fainted at parties

and let's not overlook
Ted Turner, Kim Basinger,

Mike Wallace, William Styron,
and Lauren Slater, a personal
hero of mine.

Restless nights, when anxiety
skulks by my bedside

I read the book that links
insanity and creativity,
study the ancestry of Byron,
Poe, Tennyson—

and somehow, this helps
me sleep.

Sunday Afternoon

Nick wants me to write a poem
and maybe I can do that for him—
after all, isn't it Nick who drove our car
around the corner today
just when I was feeling too weary
to ride my bicycle up the long hill ahead?

Didn't he appear out of nowhere
like a knight—yes, I mean this—
like a knight on a horse
rounding a bend
just as my legs almost gave out
under me?

Okay, it was only Sunday afternoon
in New Jersey, and I would have made it
up the hill anyway,
but didn't Nick make it easier?

Didn't he roll the car to a stop
toss me the keys
throw one leg
over the saddle and take off
toward home with his heart pumping,
lungs expanding, hips hard at work
so I could take the easy way,

the high road, the path needed
at exactly that moment?

For all the times he's done that for me
in the dozen years we've loved each other
surely I can do this much for him
surely I can do the one thing
I know I do well:
I can write it down.

Full Circle

Once

only once
when Jack was just three—

the age when my father
first took the belt to me

—once, when Jack was bouncing off the walls
when he was shouting, screaming
wouldn't keep his hands off my stereo,
telephone, radio, video camera,
answering machine

all those buttons, bells, wires, alarms,
and never-ending demands
of my hyperactive LOUD little boy
snapped something
in me

I grabbed one of those wires
he couldn't keep his hands off
maybe it was a telephone wire
or an extension cord

I ran into his room,
slammed the door

we were the only ones in the house

I slammed the door
and swung the wire over my head

but still the boy wouldn't stop

I felt my father's rage roar inside me
heard his voice in my throat
felt myself getting bigger and louder and stronger
and still Jack wouldn't stop
still he kept shouting and prancing
and bouncing off the bed
until I whipped the wire through the air
and brought it down on his back,
lashing a mark across his shoulder

he screamed
and fell down
but I wasn't finished
I climbed on top of him
still in a rage
pressed my knees into his chest
shoved my hot mouth
right into my little boy's red,
wet, snot-streaked face
and shouted, *are you afraid of me yet?*
are you afraid of me now?

The Woman Sets the Tone

The woman sets the tone in the house
—whether she weeps in the basement
screams in the attic
reads in the den

she is the metronome
the rhythm and meter
of the family.

Inside of myself
I am still an unsure girl
waiting for my mother's love

and yet I am the mother now,
I am the one who wakes and smiles
or wakes and cries

I am the woman
who catches her breath
when Melinda comes home from school
and props herself on a stool
in the kitchen.

All of this
is a wonder to me—
my place in the household,

the smooth glow on Melinda's skin,
the way she knows almost nothing
about loss or grief
but somehow is wise and kind.

What matters most to Melinda
isn't what I'm cooking
but how I look at her
when she walks into the room—

full on, even though some days
I confess some days
I am afraid
she will see
how imperfect I am
how unsteady I feel sometimes
on an ordinary day
in a not-so-ordinary way

—tell me what's on your mind today, love
talk to me about the crazy French teacher
and the boy who makes you laugh
in gym class

I don't care what you say, Melinda
I care only that you're here with me
while I'm cooking, you're here with me
in the kitchen

Melinda, the mother sets the tone
Melinda, before you go up to your room
can you tell me—

how am I doing?

If I Didn't Have Children

If I didn't have children
I wouldn't be so tired.

I'd be eating sushi
on the Upper West Side
without explaining chopsticks to anyone,
walking to a movie
with no one badgering me
about the buses
whizzing by.

If I didn't have children
I'd want them desperately.

I'd want this precise moment
in a peaceful house
with a little boy stepping from his bath,
leaving a wet shadow of his body
stamped across my clothes
when he hugs me.

If I didn't have children
I'd have no idea how it feels
to love someone so much
that birth makes you think of death
and joy makes you sad

because it won't last forever
and sunlight coming through autumn leaves
wouldn't be crystal clear in the sharing

and there wouldn't be
an 11-year-old girl next to me, saying
I remember everything—mostly it's hazy,
like a photograph that's not quite right
but beautiful anyway.

Cinderella

With his wife gone
my dad is a taller man—
forgive me, Mom
I know you carried your own burden
but you blamed each of us
at different times in our lives
you lashed out at your daughters
scowled at your husband
you scorned us
and made us smaller.

Now Dad says
some nights, after he turns off the TV
he tries to figure out what went wrong—
he wanted to save you, Mom
you were his sad, brown-eyed girl
and he was going to show you the world
he was going to make you happy

he thinks about this
in the house he built
with his own hands

he double-locks the basement door
and secures the dead bolts,
pulls on flannel pajamas

brushes his teeth
in the bathroom
he painted pink
for his bride—

he tried, Mom, I know he tried

he doesn't remember
when you had two little girls
and wanted to take us to see a movie

he doesn't remember how wounded you were
to be trapped at home, at his mercy
because you didn't know how to drive
and he didn't want to see
Walt Disney's *Cinderella*.

I think it was that day
you realized
he wouldn't save you—
no one would save you

so you learned to drive yourself
got behind the wheel
of our wood-paneled station wagon
and drove it to the grocery store
you drove it to the mall
you drove it back and forth to school

it didn't save you, Mom
it didn't make you free.

But because Dad is still alive
and because I see he is haunted
and because we all need something
to help us survive the dark hours
after midnight

I say to him,
Dad, it wasn't your fault, no one
could have made Mom happy

and for the most part
I believe it's true.

Growing Pains

Growing Pains

Melinda shot up
five inches
in seven months

passed from girl
to woman
in one lunar phase

grew hips
and all the accompaniments
that attract the gaze
of boys and men—

grown men
look at my daughter
when we walk into a room

and I am reminded
of my grandfather
who told his own daughters
all men have dirty minds,
I know, I'm a man.

What legacy
do I have
to pass on?

What wisdom,
what promise,
what charm
can I offer

that will keep her
from harm

that will carry Melinda
into the future?

Oh Boy

My son is a kindhearted boy

he's loud and bold and in your face
because the paths in his brain
are not well-worn, because
he doesn't hear the words
as you do, he hugs until it hurts
because he fears the fling
of his own intensity

Jack knows he is not well-liked
but can't figure out why.

It's about small things,
subtle cues, the way you use a pencil or
sit in your seat, the way your feet move
together in a straight line instead of
scattering around the room
bumping into people like a bull
—but a kind bull
who notices the pattern on the china
who gladly helps you set the table
even clears after supper.

My boy is big and loud
but he is kind—

what am I to tell him
about a world
that insists he learn
how to sit still
swallow a pill
fill in the dotted line?

a world
that looks at my boy
when he walks into a room
and tells him to be quiet
without giving him a chance?

a world
that can't see the good heart
behind the headstrong hurtle.

Jack Tries So Hard

When the doctor says
giving up milk and wheat
might help,
Jack leaps at the chance

he doesn't care that lasagna
will be on Nana's Christmas table,
Jack wants to start getting better
right away.

Who am I to say
no?

I am only the guardian
of his early fortune,
the bulk of life
he'll be on his own.

Pressing my hands
against his cheeks,
I promise my son
he will grow into himself

his glory days
are on the horizon.

Please, Let Me In

Melinda is cutting herself

the little girl
who never gave us
a worry in the world

cries out for help
she claims she doesn't want

sets her chin
in the clench of denial
says,

*I read about it
in a book.*

I press a sliver of glass
against my arm,
imagine the way
she describes it—

a small slice
through skin
pain
then relief
at letting something
    in.

Melinda shows me
the passage
about two girls
bloodletting together
under the bleachers

the quiet passing
of innocence
into red adolescence

I take her
to see a doctor

run my hands
along Melinda's skin,

please, let me in

pass my palms
over her firm thighs

she cries
at the rage
of invasion

says she read it
in the pages
of a book

and she's done with that
now

are we to believe her?
are we to leave her
alone in her room?

this isn't about
the disconsolation of youth

this isn't philosophy

this is not
about my mother
or about me

is it?

This is my confused child

sitting in her room
with the phone
and her books
and her door

shut.

Lies We Tell Our Children

They are so fragile

I hold them in my hands
small as I am
I am everything to them.

I'm not afraid to die

but I fear the four of us
not being together
in the event
of some calamity.

We know now
Chicken Little was right
the sky was falling
and we were the ashes

but still we tell our children

no matter what
I'll be with you

no matter what
I'll always take care of you.

What is the difference
between a lie
and what you wish
to be true?

What is a life
without the pull and pain
of truth against mercy?

How fragile
my children are to me

each of them almost lost

in a slice of broken glass
on the fringe of a crowd

alone, en masse

sometimes
it's all I can do
to think about
anything else.

Regrets

Early October,
an Indian summer afternoon
when everyone else
has gone for Italian ices
Dad stops talking about the Twin Towers
and looks across his patio
to the back hedge—

I follow his gaze, expecting
he'll say something about
the speed of the breeze
or the towers' debris

Dad has a wisp of gray hair
in his eyes, his breath comes out
in gargled sighs, he asks
do you know what I regret
most in my life?

I have some ideas of my own.
I think about his belt
on the doorknob, I think about my mother
and her sad brown eyes

my heart does a double beat
for what he might speak of

that has never been spoken between us,
what he might say
with no witness but a southerly breeze,
and the sounds of neighbors' children

smoking, he says
even though he quit
nine years ago, *if I hadn't smoked
I'd still be a healthy man*

and it makes sense,
his lungs are losing elasticity,
their capacity is shrinking

smoking, Dad says, and yes
thinking purely in terms of
personal health and consequence
it makes sense that he would regret
the box he carried Brando-style
rolled up in a T-shirt sleeve

the smoke of long-gone days
still hanging like a dirty haze
on his X ray

the bright red Marlboro lie
the cowboy legend
that lassos him now
to his chair
in the yard.

Still, Joy

At the Dining Room Table

Melinda's troubles
didn't last long

cutting was
her short-lived shot
at punk rebellion—
something
she was trying on

like red lipstick
pink hair, and safety pins

the next month Linkin Park
blink-182 and paper cuts

then skater pants
splatter jeans, pigtails

followed by UFOs
and Stephen Hawking's
meditating on time

now Melinda
plays soccer
every day

with braces on her teeth
and brown hair
blown wild—

you want some assurance
that everything will stay
okay?

we'd like that, too

but we have to settle
for Melinda at our table

eating an egg roll with chopsticks
giggling when she drops it

Melinda
filling the house with noise

running for the phone
flirting with boys

Melinda flashing
shiny silver smiles

an emerging young woman
almost an adult
and still a child.

Eye of the Self

I see it taking root in my son,
the eye of the self
squinting into the mirror
at the thick hair
his hand combs into place

the brush of gel
he leans forward
to wipe from his forehead

the white shirt
he slips over his arms, striped tie
he twists under the collar
and knots
in a rough approximation
of manhood—

all this
for a nine-year-old girl named Hillary
who wears her blond hair long,
parted on the side,
held up in one purple barrette.

For the purple barrette
a little girl
slipped into her hair

on Monday morning,
my son has showered, shampooed,
and clipped the fingernails
on his fine hands
Tuesday at dawn.

His hands
splay like puppy's paws
but I see in them
the man
reaching into the future

the man
reaching into the medicine cabinet
for toothpaste and mouthwash,
straightening his trousers,
stepping away from the mirror.

He doesn't smile
so much as tilt his head
as if hoping
to catch a glimpse of himself
from another angle,
to see himself
through Hillary's eyes

and I can tell
by the way he turns
slowly,

his shoulders sharp and straight,
that my son is satisfied

I can see
the eye of the self
in the heart of my boy
as he pulls a comb
from his back pocket
to smooth his hair
one more time.

Dear Nick,

My train ride
to the art colony
was absolutely placid

but three days here
and suddenly everything
is talking to me

I don't mean birds
but the thrum of mountains
brushed percussion of sycamores

the cleaved oak in the field
that pulled itself from the root
and endured
is singing to me, tapping me.

It's wounded, but so am I.

Anywhere else this would be insanity
everywhere else is the insistence of what's visible—
here barbed wire vibrates
with the dissonance of distant winds,
grass shifts underfoot
like shards of broken moons,
cracked bark that clings to the chestnut

is breathing the oxygen of twelve generations,
and the finch perched on a fence
is the soul of what I might become.

I wish you could have this.

What I hear is too loud for this page
what I hear is the whole alphabet
in the *x* of fallen branches
the supple *y* of growing limbs
a crescendo in the veins of leaves and cones
crumbling into carbon
that can be turned to coal
and someday shine
someday burn.

Love, L——

Thinking

I am thinking about sex
with a Mexican man
an artist
who eats sunflower seeds
while he works,
drops shells on the floor,
grinds them underfoot,
paints whole villages full of joy
and symbols that mean sex

I am thinking about a Mexican man
and he is willing
he says, *let's take off*
all our clothes
and roll down that hill,
the moon is full
it's a warm night
the ground is covered
in soft hay

I am far away
from home, no one
would ever know
I am thinking about sex
for the first time
in a long time
with someone else.

At Home

somewhere in me
is the day
we made love
on the window seat
in the middle of the afternoon
while one child
was playing soccer
and the other
was watching TV

it was spring

the air was warm
you pushed me down
and I spread open
under your
weight

years
melted away

we were younger
than we'd ever been
together

all of our history
was in your hands
on my cheeks
on my skin
under your chin

all of the love
and forgiveness

all of it
and none of it

was in your cry
as you pressed
your palm
over my mouth
and we swallowed
our own moans

then went on
with our day

in love
again
like never
before.

Stolen Beauty

I admit
I stole the flowers.
How is that different
from eating all the plums
in the icebox?

It was inspired creativity
the way I held two bunches
of yellow bud roses
in my arms
at the register
as if I meant to pay for them
while the cashier rang up cereal,
chicken wings, a package of squid
for Melinda's science project,
two cans of Spam
for the homeless.

Remember when my father
stole the salt and pepper shakers
because the restaurant
tried to pass off cubed fish
as sea scallops?
It was an act of protest,
a political statement
against exploitative pricing.

I admit
I stole the flowers,
a big bouquet of them, too.
I was practicing survival skills,
rehearsing for the possibility
of poverty in old age.

Remember Bess Myerson?
She was ensuring her future
against the collapse of Social Security
by carrying a roast beef between her thighs.

Just last year
they caught Winona Ryder
with a scarf stuffed in her pocket.
I could teach her a thing or two
about beating the feathers
out of her winter parka
to make room
for whatever meets her fancy
but personally, I think
she should be ashamed of herself,
she can afford anything
she wants.

I admit I stole the flowers,
they were pretty
and overpriced—
isn't that reason enough?

Teaching Schoolchildren
to Write About Snow

January, I am invited
into Jack's class
to talk about writing

the children bring me
a white flower
spread like a palm
over the mouth of a jelly jar vase

outside is snow
so white
it is blue,
snow that swirls
like memory
in an old woman's
milky eye

I teach the children
to write
using all five senses

(pull off your hoods
feel the world compress
tell me about your heavy boots
and soft striped scarf)

slow-moving snow
buries the hill
outside the window

for a moment
I see my mother
in knee-high boots and black coat,
pulling a sled
through streets
walled with snow—

is she smiling?

I write
that she is happy
in snow

I ask the children
to write a memory
of snow melting
as they sit near a fire
in some lovely tomorrow
unfolding and rewrapping time

I see my father
sending me back outside
barefoot
over sharp ice stones

that smell like cold metal
and blood

I run
through our dark yard
to retrieve shovels and sleds
left out to rust
in snow

my father
sends me barefoot
in my nightgown
after midnight
so I won't forget

so I remember
each time it snows—

thirty years later
while new snow
crisps white

while the flower blooms
in its jelly jar vase

while twenty faces
open toward me
dreaming snow.

Friends.com

My motorcycle boyfriend
looks me up on the Internet
after twenty years
he turns the camera on himself,
clicks without even combing his hair
says he wants to talk over old times.

My college roommate,
one of the girls
with closets full of jeans,
sends a Christmas card
and photo of her kids.

It seems everyone
wants to apologize
for how they treated me
in years gone by.

I tell them thanks
but there's no room for you
in this life.

Ordinary

Is it dull
to have an ordinary life
or is it glorious?

I think it depends on the day
and what you think is ordinary

and how true
is your love.

Today
in the newspaper
I read that scientists
say the very same stars
that exploded at the origin of time
have found their way
into the fibers
of our skin.

After breakfast
I walked out
with the dog

and asked myself
is anyone
or anything
truly ordinary?

Stars die
and life begins

every possibility
is in us
at this very moment—
how can a day
be ordinary?

I feared
beyond reason
that I would lose my mind
or grow to know
my mother's misery
in the intimate way
we know the sound
of our own blood

and I am not lost
I am not miserable—
how can a day
be ordinary?

How can a day
be ordinary
when the orbit of planets
in the vacuum of sky
mirrors the movement
of molecules?

What's in the heavens,
too large for us to see,
is in our selves,
too minuscule to witness.

If we stand still
we can feel infinity
in our limbs—

if I stand still
the dog tugs at her leash
and the cold
lashes my skin

so I go inside,
wash the breakfast dishes,
make the beds, read a book,
simmer veal for stew

I put dinner on the table,
summon my family to the kitchen,
and call it ordinary
when two or more
of the people I love
gather in the same room

we call it ordinary
even as stars
spin inside us.

Fate

The Sirens

There was a fate for me

I would marry a man
who worked with his hands
buy a small place in Levittown
maybe move out to Commack
make the house bigger
put on a dormer
fill it with colonial furniture
plastic flowers
two children or more

you could do worse
I was told
I would cook
I would cook
I would cook
and drive a station wagon

take vacations
in a pop-up camper
pack the car with suitcases,
sand, wet bathing suits
souvenirs

avoid the borders
pay my bills on time

join a bowling team
take a part-time job
barbecue with other couples

pretend
to be happy—

this was the fate
my sirens were singing
I heard them wailing day and night
from the jailhouse behind our school
telling me where I belonged.

Some folks say
in the land of opportunity
the starting line doesn't matter
but let me ask

what was expected of you
at the age of fifteen?
how wide was your horizon?
where were you destined?
who set the course?
what were you told to dream
of? how far was too far
to imagine? what joy
was yours to attain?

There was a fate for me.

Hurry

Looking back
I can see my whole life
was about moving away
from pain

I wasn't running
from myself
but from the pain
of myself

time was my enemy
even as a little girl
I knew it could run out
before I'd outraced
the loud noise
of my demons

if I didn't get away in time
I'd be trapped
in that place of pain
for life

like my mother
who gave up early
then thwarted my efforts
with disgusted sneers

someday, I hissed at her,
someday I'm going to be out there
in the world
and you'll still be stuck
in these same four walls

now she's in her grave
there's no satisfaction
in hearing my words
ring true through time

but understanding
why I ran so hard
why my heart raced
at two in the morning
when I woke
and heard the kitchen clock
ticking—

that matters to me

it explains my galloping flight
the free-fall fright
of running through years
as fast as I could

my father asking,
why are you in such a hurry?
my mother pressing her lips together
because she knew.

Epilogue

Moon over New York

My father looks at the moon
and wonders if I am looking at it, too.

Can you imagine
the man who threw me down
the basement stairs
sent me barefoot into the snow
beat red stripes into my legs
and locked me out of the house
loves me so much now

that he pumps oxygen
into his fragile lungs
opens his front door
looks up at the night sky

and a hundred miles away
in my own backyard
I think of him
while I watch the moon
wane and fade
   disappear

and come back again
and again and
again.

Author's Note

Each of us has a tale we tell ourselves
in order to survive.

This is my tale.

All names and some factual details
have been modified
to satisfy literary license
and to protect people's privacy.

Every word is absolutely true in spirit.

Acknowledgments

I gratefully acknowledge
the generous support
necessary encouragement
and reckless faith
of the following people
and institutions:

Frank Albanese
John Albanese
Mary Albanese
Melissa Albanese
Larry Ashmead
Amy Becker
Kelly Belloli
Nadine Billard
Alison Callahan
Geraldine R. Dodge Foundation
Jennifer Hart
Rosemarie Helm
Rosanne Joos
Donna Lico
Toni Martin
Angela Miller
Laura Morowitz
Jed Rosen
Emily Rosenblum
Jennifer Sheridan
Virginia Center for the Creative Arts
Susan Weinberg

This book
is dedicated
to my father,

Larry Lico
1932–2002

he taught me to endure
and I never doubted
his love.

This book
is also dedicated
to my mother,

Bobbie Lico
1940–1993

her soul
was still emerging

and wherever she is
in the universe
I wish her
joy.